For Torben, with love
~ M.C.B.

To Jack Aldridge Palmer
~ T.M.

tiger tales
5 River Road, Suite 128, Wilton, CT 06897
Published in the United States 2020
Originally published in Great Britain 2020
by Little Tiger Press Ltd.
Text copyright © 2020 M. Christina Butler
Illustrations copyright © 2020 Tina Macnaughton
ISBN-13: 978-1-68010-212-3
ISBN-10: 1-68010-212-5
Printed in China
LTP/1800/1337/0420
10 9 8 7 6 5 4 3 2 1

For more insight and activities,
visit us at www.tigertalesbooks.com

One Christmas Wish

by M. Christina Butler • *Illustrated by* Tina Macnaughton

tiger tales

Little Hedgehog and his friends were
having a snack when a flurry of snow
fluttered past the window.

"It's going to be a white Christmas!"
said Rabbit excitedly.

"Yippee!" squeaked the baby mice.
"We can build snow mice!"

"Let's make them together! Come
over tomorrow, everyone," suggested
Little Hedgehog.

But the next day, the snow had melted.
"It's all gone!" cried the baby mice.
"We can't build snow mice without snow,"
grumbled Fox.

"Don't worry!" replied Little Hedgehog kindly.
"Look, there's some snow on those branches
and a little under that bush. If we collect
it in my hat, we'll have enough in no time!"
"A snow hunt!" they all cheered.

"We wish you a Merry
Christmas," everyone sang
as they searched through the
woods and up Rocky Ridge, collecting
snow along the way.

When they reached the very top,
they found a blanket
of glistening snow.
"Let's make snow
angels!" laughed
Rabbit, diving in.

They all scooped the snow into Little
Hedgehog's hat until it was full to the brim.
    Then Badger declared, "Time to head back!"
and off they went.

They were halfway home when they passed
Grandpa Squirrel decorating his tree.
"Can we help?" offered Little Hedgehog.
"Oh, thank you!" smiled Grandpa Squirrel.

When the last ornament was in place,
the friends stepped back to admire the tree.
   "It still doesn't look very Christmassy,"
sighed Grandpa Squirrel. "Something's
missing."
   The baby mice knew exactly
what it was . . . .

"What a fun Christmas
Eve this is turning into,"
smiled Little Hedgehog
as the friends set off.

"You need some snow
to frost the needles!"
they announced.
"Perfect!" beamed
Grandpa Squirrel.
"How kind you are!"

Near the riverbank, they found the Beavers looking glum.
"We planned a winter snowball fight," they explained,
"but the snow melted!"
The baby mice rushed over to the snow-filled hat.
"We have just the thing . . . ," they chuckled.

"Ready, set . . . snowball fight!" yelled
a baby mouse, throwing the first snowball.
They passed out handfuls of snow, and
everyone joined in.

"My goodness!" exclaimed Rabbit, looking up. "We'd better head home before it gets dark."

"Race you back!" called Fox, bounding off into the woods.

But Fox hadn't gotten far when . . .

. . ."OUCH!"

He tripped and landed with a bump.

"Oh, dear, that foot does look sore," said
Badger, taking a closer look. "But nothing
a cold compress can't fix!"

"We can use our snow!" called
the baby mice.

With the hat fastened around
Fox's foot, and Badger and
Rabbit by his side, the friends
walked slowly back to
Little Hedgehog's
house.

"Time for hot chocolate!" said
Badger when they arrived.

"And we can build our snow mice!"
giggled the baby mice. But when they
peeked inside Little Hedgehog's hat . . .

. . . the very last flake was melting at the bottom!
"Our snow!" cried the baby mice. "It's all
gone! Christmas won't be special without it."

Mouse hugged them close.
"You've already made
Christmas special," she said,
"by sharing your snow."

"Our snow did bring a lot of happiness,"
they sniffed.
"And Christmas isn't over yet!" added
Little Hedgehog, waving good-bye.
"Come back tomorrow, and we'll
all celebrate together!"

That evening, Little Hedgehog thought about the baby mice.

"They were so kind to give away their snow," he sighed. "There must be a way to make their Christmas wish come true."

Suddenly, he had an idea. All through the night, he painted and glued . . .

folded and snipped, until his
surprise was finally ready.

On Christmas Day, Little Hedgehog's
house was a wonderland of pine cones
and sparkling snowflakes.

"Thank you! It's magical!" cheered the baby mice. "But there's something even MORE magical . . . ."

"What's that?" smiled Little Hedgehog.

"Spending Christmas with all our friends!" they laughed as fresh flakes of snow fluttered past the window.